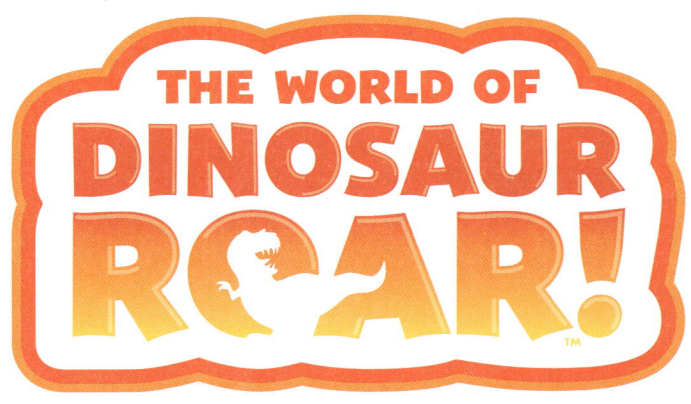

SQUEAK SEEKS!

**The World of Dinosaur Roar!™
created by Peter Curtis**
Based on *Dinosaur Roar!* by Paul Stickland and Henrietta Stickland

In Collaboration with the Smithsonian Institution

National Museum of Natural History
Matthew T. Miller, Museum Specialist

For Smithsonian Enterprises:
Avery Naughton, Licensing Coordinator
Paige Towler, Editorial Lead
Jill Corcoran, Senior Director, Licensed Publishing
Brigid Ferraro, Vice President of New Business and Licensing
Carol LeBlanc, President

For The Dinosaur Roar Company:
Nick Barrington, President

SIMON SPOTLIGHT
An imprint of Simon & Schuster Children's Publishing Division
1230 Avenue of the Americas, New York, New York 10020
For more than 100 years, Simon & Schuster has championed authors and the stories they create.
By respecting the copyright of an author's intellectual property, you enable Simon & Schuster and the author to continue publishing exceptional books for years to come. We thank you for supporting the author's copyright by purchasing an authorized edition of this book.
This Simon Spotlight edition May 2025
The World of Dinosaur Roar! created by Peter Curtis
Inspired by *Dinosaur Roar!* by Paul Stickland and Henrietta Stickland.
Text: Peter Curtis and Patty Michaels. Text and illustrations copyright © The Dinosaur Roar Company Ltd. 2025.
Dinosaur Roar! and *The World of Dinosaur Roar!* are trademarks of The Dinosaur Roar Company Limited.
Dinosaur facts verified by Matthew T. Miller of the Department of Paleobiology, the Smithsonian National Museum of Natural History.
The name Smithsonian is a registered trademark of the Smithsonian Institution.
The Smithsonian is the world's largest museum and research complex, dedicated to public education, national service, and scholarship in the arts, Smithsonian sciences, and history.
For more information, please visit www.si.edu
All rights reserved, including the right of reproduction in whole or in part in any form.
SIMON SPOTLIGHT, READY-TO-READ, and colophon are registered trademarks of Simon & Schuster, LLC.
For information about special discounts for bulk purchases, please contact Simon & Schuster Special Sales at 1-866-506-1949 or business@simonandschuster.com.
Simon & Schuster strongly believes in freedom of expression and stands against censorship in all its forms.
For more information, visit BooksBelong.com.
Manufactured in the United States of America 0325 LAK
10 9 8 7 6 5 4 3 2 1
ISBN 9781665971768 (hc)
ISBN 9781665971751 (pbk)
ISBN 9781665971775 (ebook)

SQUEAK SEEKS!

By Peter Curtis and Patty Michaels

Ready-to-Read

Simon Spotlight
New York   Amsterdam/Antwerp   London
Toronto   Sydney/Melbourne   New Delhi

This is Dinosaur Squeak. Squeak is a *Compsognathus* (say: Comp-sog-NATH-us).

Squeak is one of the smallest dinosaurs.

Today Dinosaur Squeak is going on an adventure in the forest.

Squeak likes to seek!
What will Squeak find?

Squeak finds a log to crawl through. That was fun!

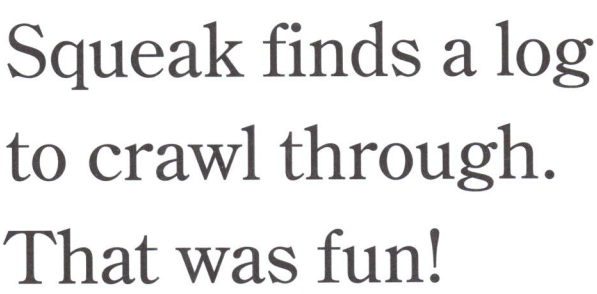

Squeak spots things she has never seen before.

They are brown and hard.
They have scales.

They are pine cones!

Next, Squeak sees a trail of ants walking in a straight line.

Squeak counts them.
There are twelve ants!

Squeak hops on top of a huge pile of rocks.

She spots pretty flowers on the ground.

Then, Squeak sees a group of plants. They are so green!

A little while later, Squeak gets tired.

She rests on a tree stump.

Soon, Squeak is ready to play again!

She slides across
a slippery leaf.
Whee!

Then Squeak sees another dinosaur in the forest.

It is Dinosaur Munch!

Munch is a *Diplodocus* (say: DIP-low-DOCK-us).

Munch is hungry.
As he tries to
suck up leaves
to eat, Squeak gets
sucked in, too!

Squeak decides to look for more dinosaur friends.

Squeak spots a dinosaur behind some rocks.
It is Dinosaur Roar!

Roar is a *Tyrannosaurus rex* (say: Tie-RAN-oh-sore-us rex).

Squeak is so happy to see Roar.

Squeak had such a great day seeking! Can you remember all the things Squeak found?

Learn some more fun facts about *Compsognathus*!

- The word **Compsognathus** means "elegant jaw."
- It was one of the smallest dinosaurs and only about the size of a chicken.
- It had a very long tail that it held off the ground, and it walked on the tips of its toes rather than the flat of its foot.
- It had a long, flexible neck that helped it better search for food. It also had long arms, each ending in three-fingered claw hands.
- This dinosaur had a mouth full of small, sharp, curved teeth, and ate mainly insects and lizards.
- It had a narrow head that went to a point at its snout.